HATTIE the BAD

Jane Devlin

Joe Berger

PUFFIN

To my
mum and dad
— J.D.

For my sister,
Hattie the fab
— J.B.

PUFFIN BOOKS
Published by the Penguin Group: London, New York,
Australia, Canada, India, Ireland, New Zealand and South Africa
Penguin Books Ltd, Registered Offices:
80 Strand, London WC2R 0RL, England

puffinbooks.com

First published 2009
1 3 5 7 9 10 8 6 4 2
Text copyright © Jane Devlin, 2009
Illustrations copyright © Joe Berger, 2009
All rights reserved
The moral right of the author and illustrator has been asserted
Printed in China
ISBN: 978–0–141–50235–9

HATTIE was BAD.

When I say **BAD**, I don't mean forgot-to-tidy-her-room, reading-comics-after-bedtime kind of **BAD**.

When I say **BAD**,

I mean **really,** really BAD.

That

is why

she was called

HATTIE THE
BAD

Hattie's mum said that Hattie had
always been a *good* baby until one day she

dropped
her on her
head.

But even Hattie's baby brother Osric could have told you that was a **load** of baloney.

Baby 20p

Spider (angry) 5p

Bunny 5p

Ball 20p

The truth of the matter was,
when Hattie was a tiny, little girl
she had actually been

quite good.

But after a while, she couldn't
help noticing that being **good** meant
you had to do rubbish things like
eating mushy food and going to
bed when you weren't even tired.

And **where** was the fun in that?

Exactly.

So Hattie became **BAD.**

At first she could only do small bad things like
eating dog biscuits, even though
they didn't taste nice.

But as she got older, she got better and better at it.

You might be thinking that as Hattie was so **BAD**
she wouldn't have any friends, but you would be wrong.
As Hattie was always doing exciting **BAD** things,
the other children thought she was great.

Their parents disagreed.

They told their children not to play with Hattie.
Being **BAD** with no one else to enjoy
it made Hattie feel **sad**.

So she had an idea:

Hattie the Good.

She would be just as **good**
at being **good** as she
had been at being **BAD.**

So,
she
wore
whatever
her
mother
wanted.

She
kept her
room
tidy.

She even went to
bed without being asked.

Soon the other parents forgot about
Hattie the **BAD**.

"Sit next to Hattie,"
they said. "She always
gets the **best** marks."

"I don't know why
you're complaining,
Hattie looks **lovely**
in hers."

Soon the children got so fed up
they didn't want to play with Hattie anyway.

Word spread and
one day some reporters
came and filmed Hattie
at school.

Then a letter
came inviting her
to a competition to find

The
BEST-BEHAVED
CHILD
Ever!

The day came.
The *famous teevee lady*
had a large **golden** envelope.

She opened
it up . . .

Winner!

Suddenly Hattie got a **funny** feeling inside.

As she walked up the stairs, the feeling got bigger and bigger.

¨KNIC

KERS!"

as **loud** as

she possibly

could.

All over the country grown-ups **gasped** and tried to cover their children's ears.

All over the country children, even the good ones, **cheered.**

HATTIE THE **BAD** was **back**.

And **no one** refused to play with her . . .

ever again.